SAY HELLO TO MY LITTLE FRIEND!

THE QUOTABLE SCARFACE™

Edited by Michael McAvennie

Based on the Universal Motion Picture

POCKET BOOKS

New York London Toronto Syndey

POCKET BOOKS, a division of Simon & Schuster, Inc.
1230 Avenue of the Americas, New York, NY 10020

First Pocket Books trade paperback edition September 2007

POCKET and colophon are registered trademarks of Simon & Schuster Inc.

For information regarding special discounts for bulk purchases, please contact:
Simon & Schuster Special Sales at 1.800.456.6798 or business@simonandschuster.com

Designed by Jan Pisciotta

Manufactured in the United States of America

10 9 8 7 6 5 4 3 2

ISBN–13: 978-1-4165-4714-3
ISBN–10: 1-4165-4714-2

The Self-Aware

SCARFACE™

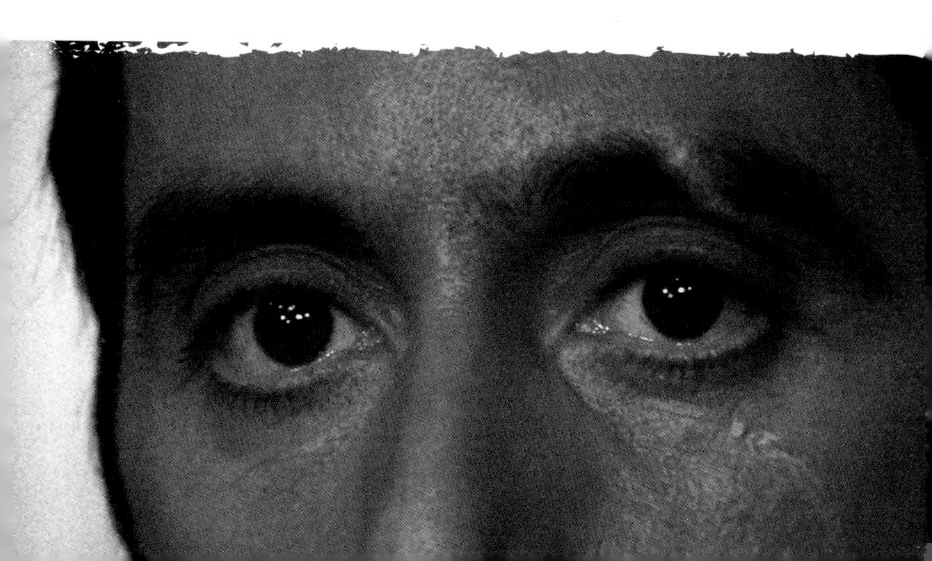

TONY:

"I'm no f#@%in' criminal, man.
I'm no **puta of a thief**.
I'm *Tony Montana*, a political
prisoner from Cuba. And I want my
f#@%ing 'human rights' **now!**"

OMAR: "Gotta unload a boat. **Marijuana.** Twenty-five tons. You get five hundred each."

MANNY: "Five hundred, eh? That's great, eh?"

TONY: "You gotta be kidding.... Who do you think we are? **Baggage handlers**?"

HECTOR: "Where you from, Tony?"

TONY: "What the f#@% difference does it make where I'm from, man?"

HECTOR: "*¡Coño! Cogelo.* Take it easy, man. I, uh, I just want to get to know who I do business with."

TONY: "You'll get to know me once you start doing business with me and stop f#@%ing around, Hector."

TONY: "Hey, Sosa.... I never f#@%ed anybody over in my life didn't have it coming to him, **you got that?** All I have in this world is *my balls* and *my word*, and I don't break 'em for *no one*, **you understand?**"

SOSA: “I think you speak from the heart, Montana.”

IMMIGRATION OFFICER: "Been in a **mental** hospital?"

TONY: "**Oh yeah**, in the boat coming over."

ELVIRA: "What makes you so much **better** than me? What do you do? You deal drugs and you **kill** people. Oh, that's wonderful, Tony. ***Real*** **contribution** to human history!"

TONY: **"You need people like me,
so you can point your f#@%ing fingers
and say 'That's the bad guy!'
So what that make you? Good?
You just know how to hide—and lie.
Me, I don't have that problem. Me, I
always tell the truth, even
when I lie."**

"So say good night to the bad guy! Come on! The last time you gonna see a bad guy like this again, let me tell you!"

TONY: "Who the f#@% you think I am, your f#@%in' bellboy?! You wanna go to war? You wanna go to war? We take you to war, okay?!"

TONY:
"Who you think you f#@%in'
with?! I TONY MONTANA!
You f#@% with me, you f#@%in'
with the BEST!"

TONY: “Mr. Lopez. It’s a real pleasure.”

LOPEZ: “You can call me ‘FRANK.’ Everybody calls me ‘FRANK.’ My Little League team. Even the f#@%ing prosecutors around town, they *all* call me ‘FRANK.’ ”

The Opportunistic

SCARFACE™

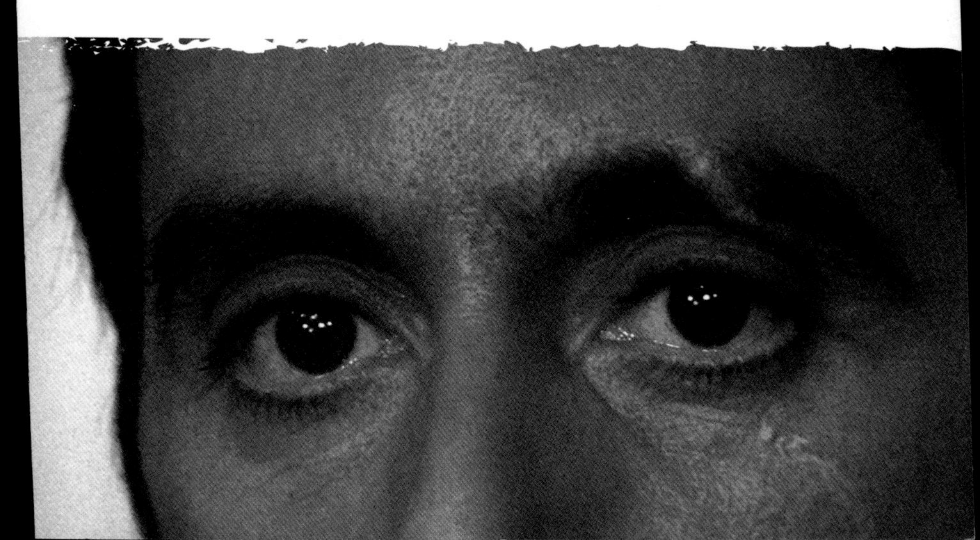

TONY:

"*¡Coño!* Lookit this. **F#@%in' onions.** I oughta be pickin' gold from the street."

LOPEZ: "You stay loyal in this business, you're gonna move up. You gonna move up fast.... And then you're gonna find out your **biggest problem** is not bringing in the stuff, but what to do with all the f#@%ing cash!"

TONY: **"I hope I have that problem sometime."**

MANNY: "I say be happy with what you got."

TONY: "*You* be happy. **Me, I want what's coming to me.**"

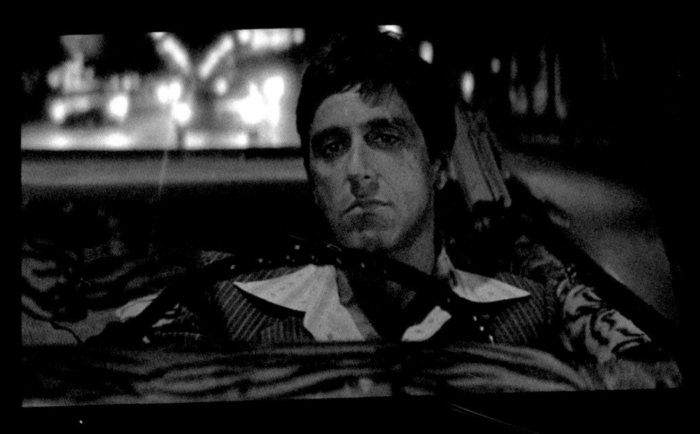

MANNY: "Well, what's comin' to you, Tony?"

TONY: "**The world,** *chico*. And everything in it."

COOK: **"Hey, hey, what you guys doing? There's a lot of dishes to be washed!"**

TONY: **"Wash 'em yourself, man. I retire!"**

COOK: **"What the f#@% you gonna do then now?"**

TONY: **"I gotta look after my investment!"**

LOPEZ: **"It comes down to one thing, Tony boy, and you never forget. Lesson number one: Don't underestimate the other guy's greed!"**

ELVIRA: **"Lesson number two: Don't get high on your own supply."**

TONY: **"What I try to tell you? This country, you gotta make the money first. Then when you get the money, you get the power. Then when you get the power, *then* you get the woman. That's why you gotta make your own moves."**

SOSA: "I think you and me . . . we do business together a long time. Just **remember**, I'll only tell you one time: don't f#@% me, Tony. **Don't you ever try to f#@% me.**"

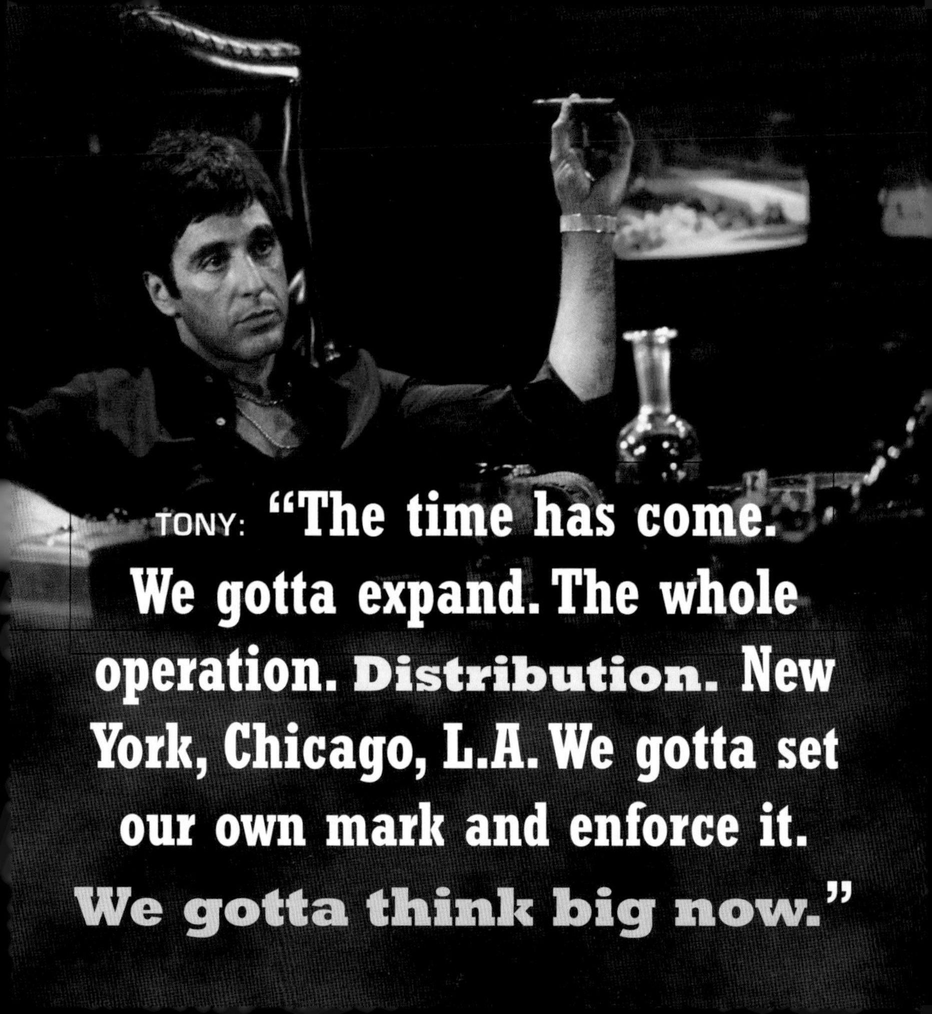

TONY: "The time has come. We gotta expand. The whole operation. **Distribution.** New York, Chicago, L.A. We gotta set our own mark and enforce it. **We gotta think big now.**"

TONY:

"Here's to the land of **opportunity.**"

ELVIRA:

"For ***you***, maybe."

The Practical

SCARFACE™

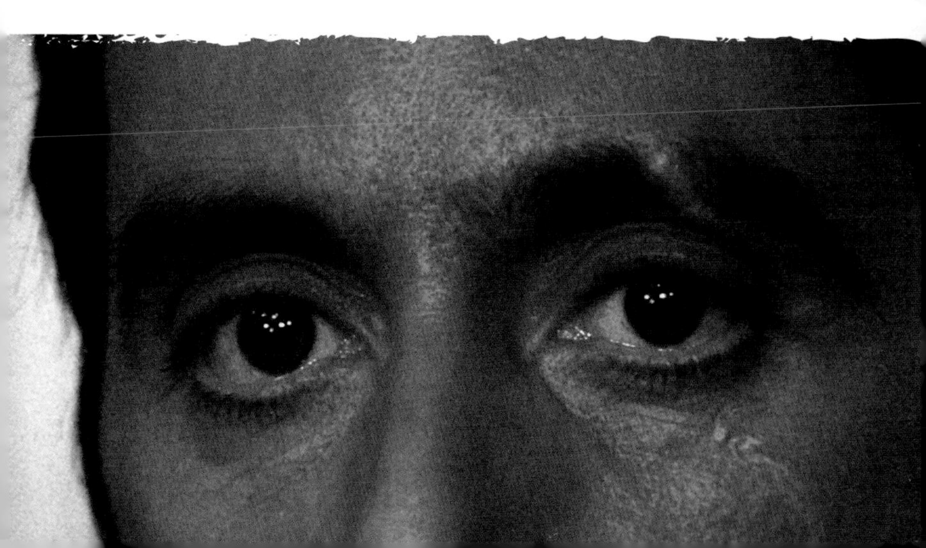

TONY:

"You a Communist? Huh? How'd you like it, man? They tell you all the time what to do, what to think, what to feel. You wanna be like a sheep? Like all those other people, man? Baah. Baah."

TONY: "You tell your guys in Miami—your friend—it be a pleasure. **I kill a Communist for fun,** but for a green card, I gonna carve him up **real nice.**"

TONY: **"I'm working with an anti-Castro group. I'm an organizer now, and I get a lot of political contributions."**

MAMA: **"Sure you do. A gun sticking in somebody's face is how."**

BERNSTEIN:

"The word on the street, Tony, is you're bringing in a lot of *yeyo*. That means you're not a small-time punk anymore. You're public property now. Supreme Court says that your privacy can be invaded."

TONY:

"Okay, how much?"

TONY: "So . . . what am I looking at here?"

SHEFFIELD: "Five years. You'll be out in three. Maybe less, if I can **make a deal.**"

TONY: "Three f#@%in' years! **For *what?!*** Washing money? The f#@%in' country was ***built*** on washed money!"

TONY:

"You know what capitalism is? Getting f#@%ed."

The Romantic

SCARFACE™

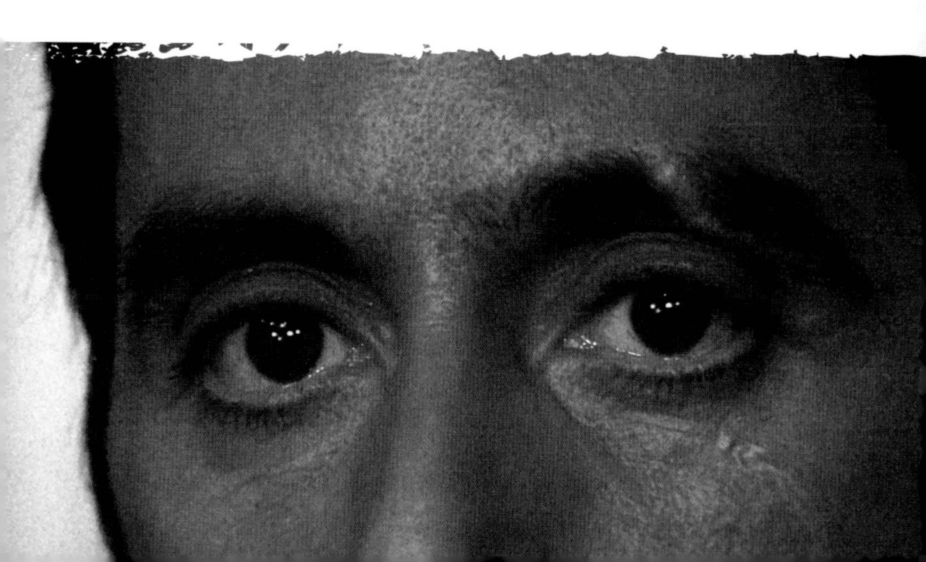

LOPEZ: "Where the hell's Elvira already? . . . F#@%ing broad! She spends half her life dressing, the other half, **undressing.**"

TONY:
"Gotta get her **in between.**"

TONY: "You're good-looking. You got a beautiful body, beautiful legs, a beautiful face, all these guys in love with you. Only you **got a look in your eye** like you haven't been f#@%ed in a year."

ELVIRA: "Hey, Jose, who, why, when, and how I f#@% is **none of your business,** okay?"

TONY: "Now you're talking to me, baby! **That I like, okay!** Keep it coming, baby!"

ELVIRA: "Even if I were blind, **desperate**, starved, and begging for it on a desert island, *you'd* be the **last thing** I'd ever **f#@%.**"

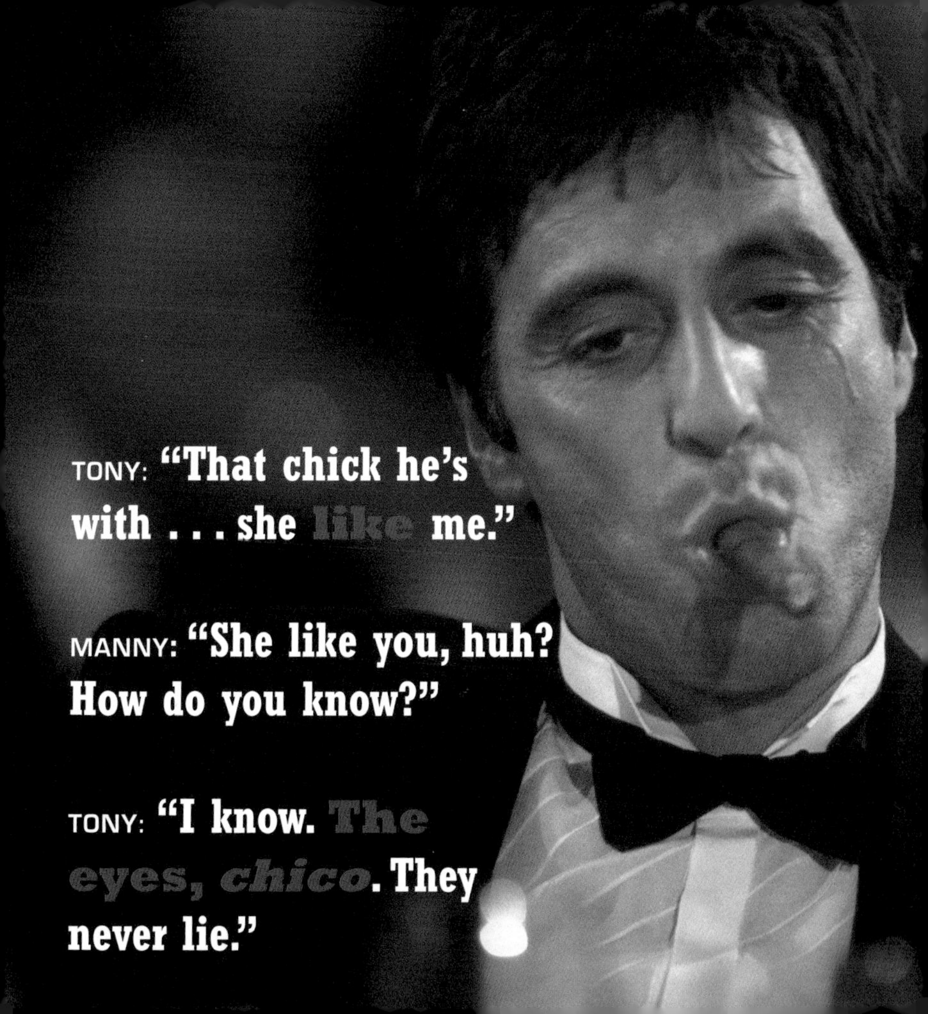

TONY: "That chick he's with . . . she like me."

MANNY: "She like you, huh? How do you know?"

TONY: "I know. The eyes, *chico*. They never lie."

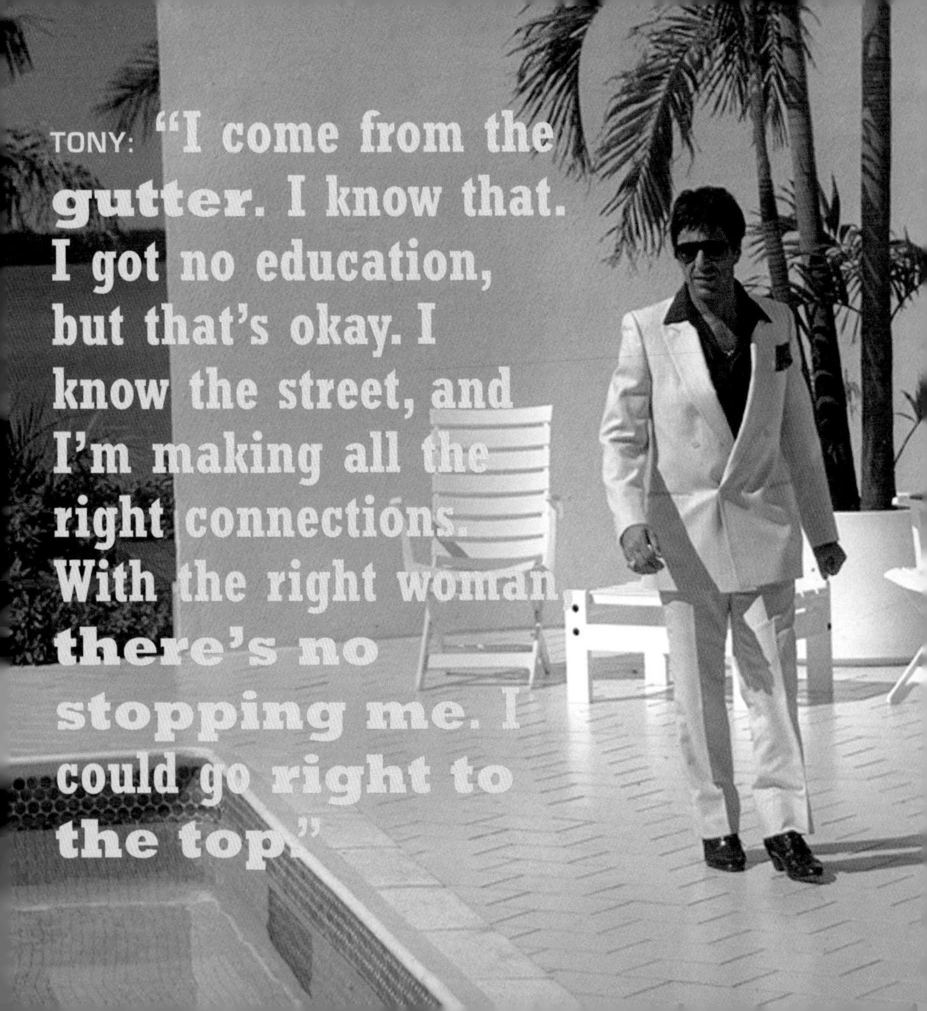

TONY: "I come from the **gutter**. I know that. I got no education, but that's okay. I know the street, and I'm making all the right connections. With the right woman, **there's no stopping me.** I could go **right to the top.**"

ELVIRA: "You're an **immigrant spic millionaire** who can't stop talking about how much money he's got, or how he's getting f#@%ed. . . ."

TONY: "Who the **f#@%** you callin' a **spic**, you **white piece of bread**? Get out of the way of the television!"

TONY: "Why don't you get a job or something, you know? Do something. Be a nurse. Work with blind kids, lepers, that kind of thing. Anything beats lying around all day waiting for me to f#@% you, I tell you that."

ELVIRA: **“Don’t toot your horn, honey. You’re not that good.”**

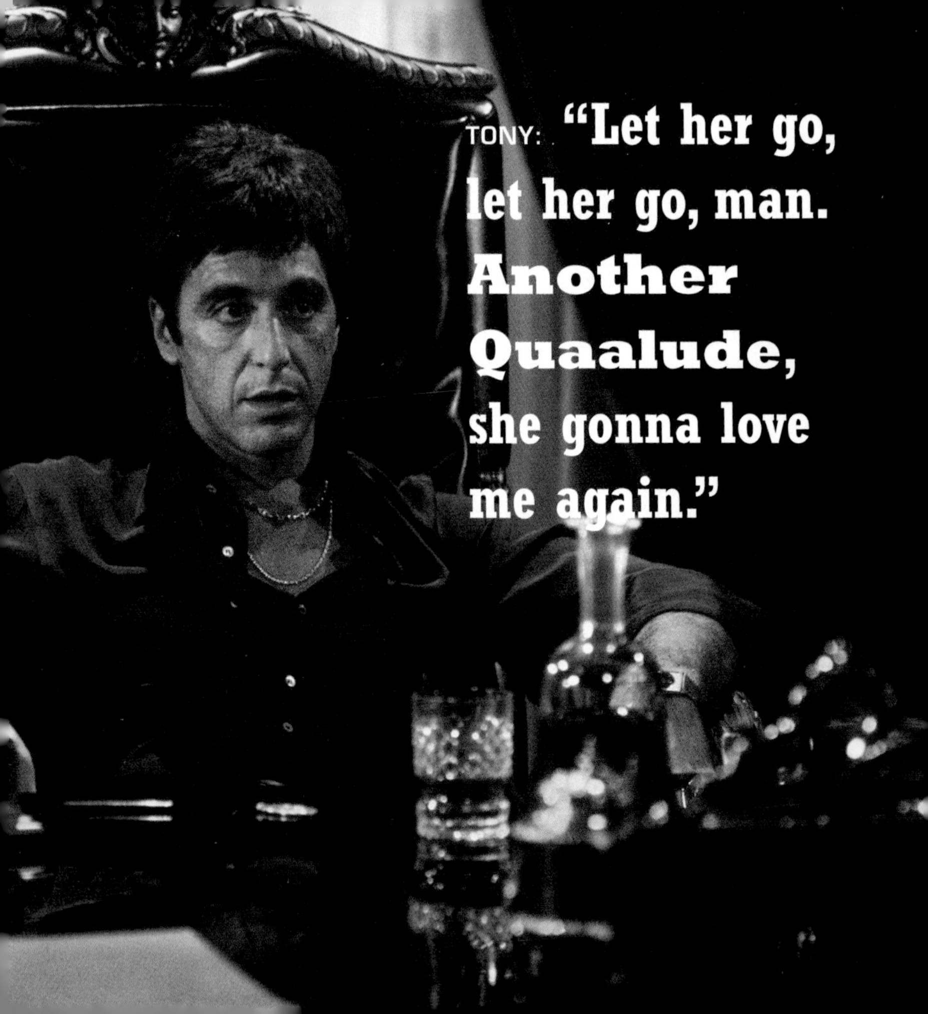
TONY: "Let her go, let her go, man. Another Quaalude, she gonna love me again."

The Vengeful

SCARFACE™

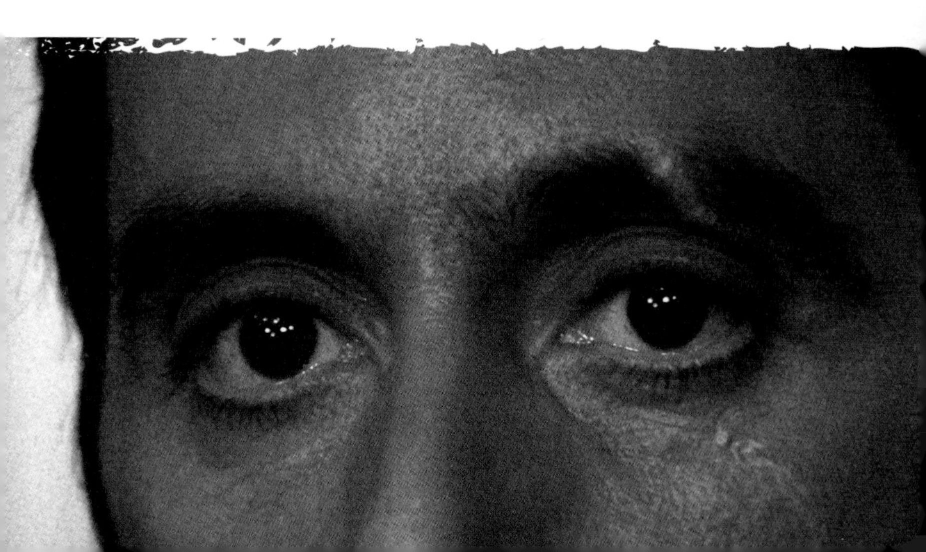

IMMIGRATION OFFICER: **“Where’d you get that beauty scar, tough guy? Eatin’ p#@%y?”**

TONY: **“How am I gonna get a scar like that eating p#@%y, man? This was when I was a kid, you know? You should see the other kid. You can’t recognize him.”**

TONY: "Frog face, you just f#@%ed yourself. You steal from me, you're dead."

CHI-CHI: **"What we gonna do now?"**

TONY: **"Do? We're going to *war*. That's what we're gonna do. We gonna eat that Sosa for breakfast . . . close that f#@%er down."**

TONY: **"DIE! DIE!"**

TONY:

"No, I **not** all right! I'm pissed, you know! And when I get back there, I **gonna kick some ass** all over the f#@%in' place!"

TONY
"Okay! You
wanna play rough?
Okay!

SAY HELLO TO MY
LITTLE
END!

LOPEZ: **"Tony, no, don't kill me, please . . ."**

TONY: **"I won't kill you. . . . *Manolo*, shoot that piece of s@%t."**

The Unambiguous

SCARFACE™

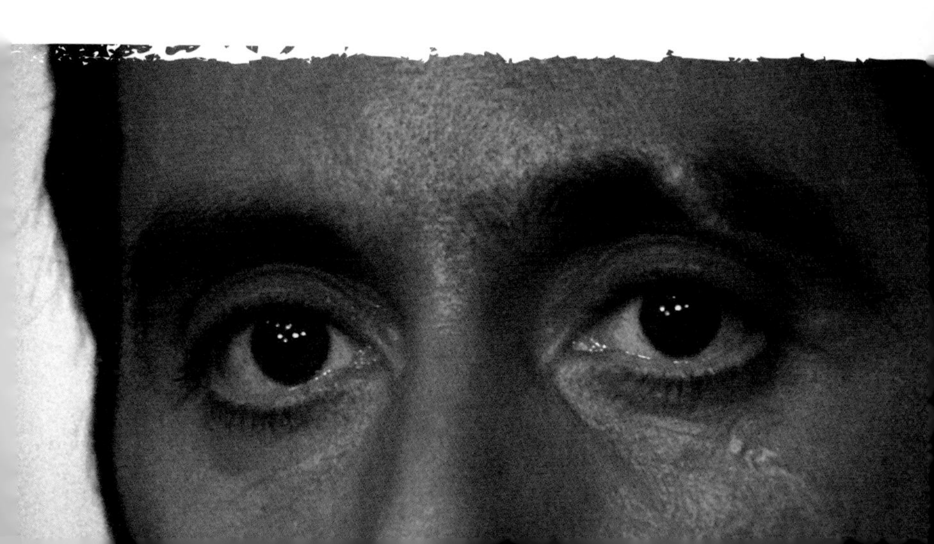

HECTOR: "You want to give me the cash . . . or I **kill** your brother first, before I **kill** you?"

TONY: "Why don't you try sticking your head up **your ass**? See if it **fits**."

MANNY: "Man, that's the boss's lady, okay? You're gonna get us **killed**."

TONY: "F#@% you, man. . . . That guy's **soft**. Look in his face. The booze and the *cuncha* tell him what to do."

LOPEZ: "What do you think of him?"

OMAR: **"I think he's a f#@%ng peasant!"**

LOPEZ: "Yeah . . . but you get a guy **like that** on your side, he breaks his back for you."

ELVIRA:

"I wouldn't be **caught dead** in that thing. . . . It looks like somebody's ***nightmare.***"

TONY: "Looking good, Ernie. Keep up the bad work."

TONY: "F#@% Gaspar Gomez, and f#@% the f#@%ing Diaz brothers! **F#@% 'em all!** I bury those **cockroaches**! What did they ever do for **us**?!"

The Philosophical SCARFACE™

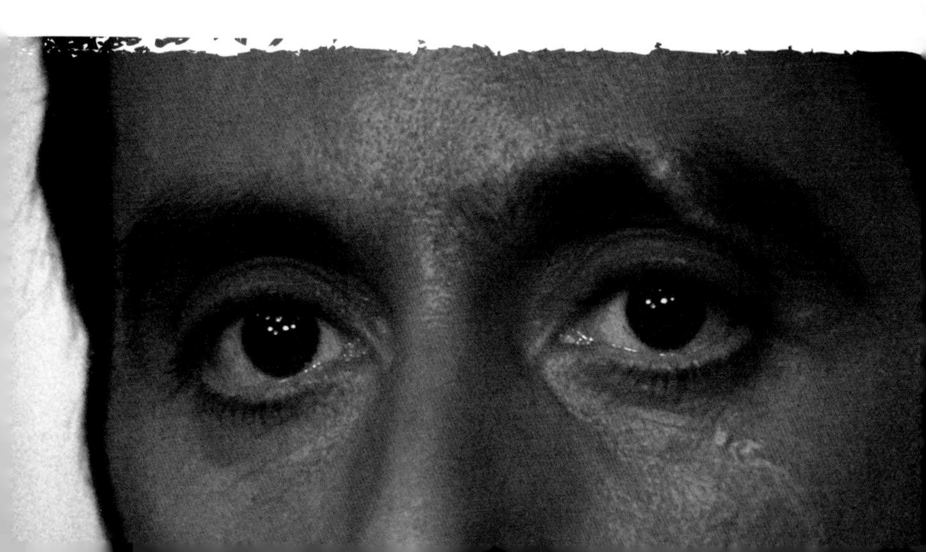

TONY: "This is **paradise**, I'm tellin' you. This town is like a **great, big p#@%y** just waitin' to get f#@%ed."

BERNSTEIN: "You oughta **smile** more, Tony. You gotta enjoy yourself. Every day **above ground** is a good day."

TONY: **"Orders? *You* giving *me* orders? *Amigo,* the only one thing in this world that gives orders is *balls,* okay? *Balls.*"**

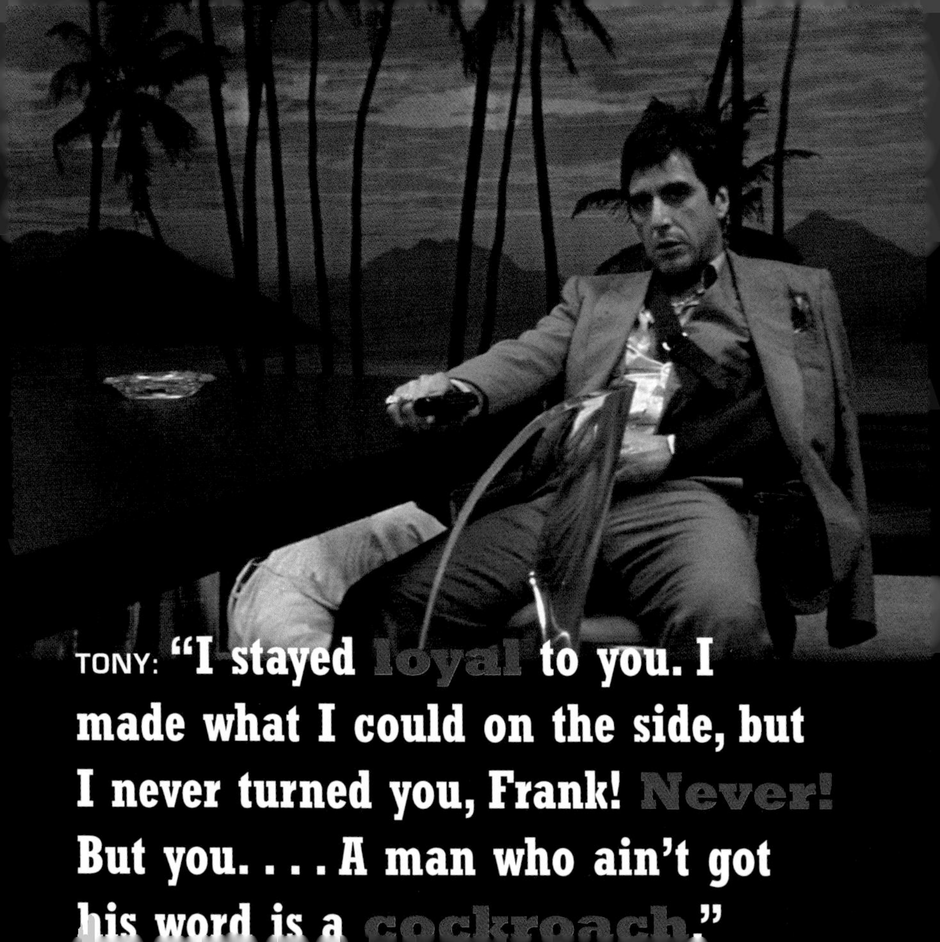
TONY: “I stayed loyal to you. I
made what I could on the side, but
I never turned you, Frank! Never!
But you. . . . A man who ain’t got
his word is a cockroach.”

ELVIRA: "Nothing exceeds like excess."

TONY:

“Who put this thing together? *ME!* That’s who! Who do I trust? *ME!*”

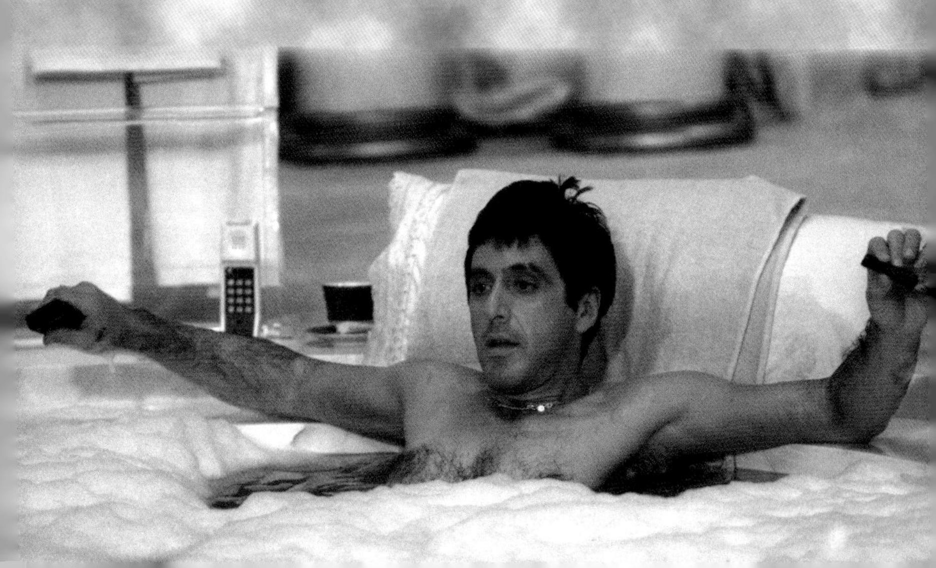

TONY: **"Is this it? This what it's all about, Manny? Eating . . . drinking . . . f#@%ing . . . sucking . . . snorting? Then what?"**

The Untouchable

SCARFACE™

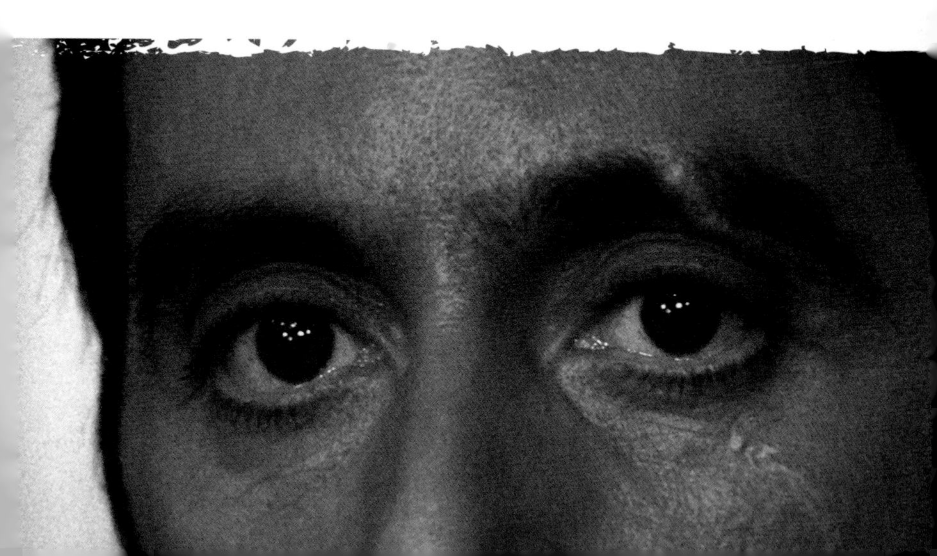

ELVIRA: "You know, Frank, if anyone ever wanted to **assassinate** you, you wouldn't be too hard to find."

LOPEZ: "Assassinate **me**? Who the hell would want to kill me? I got nothing but friends."

ELVIRA: "You **never** know, do you? Maybe the catcher on your Little League team."

LOPEZ: "The catcher? That **son of a bitch**, he didn't get a base hit all season! I should kill **him**!"

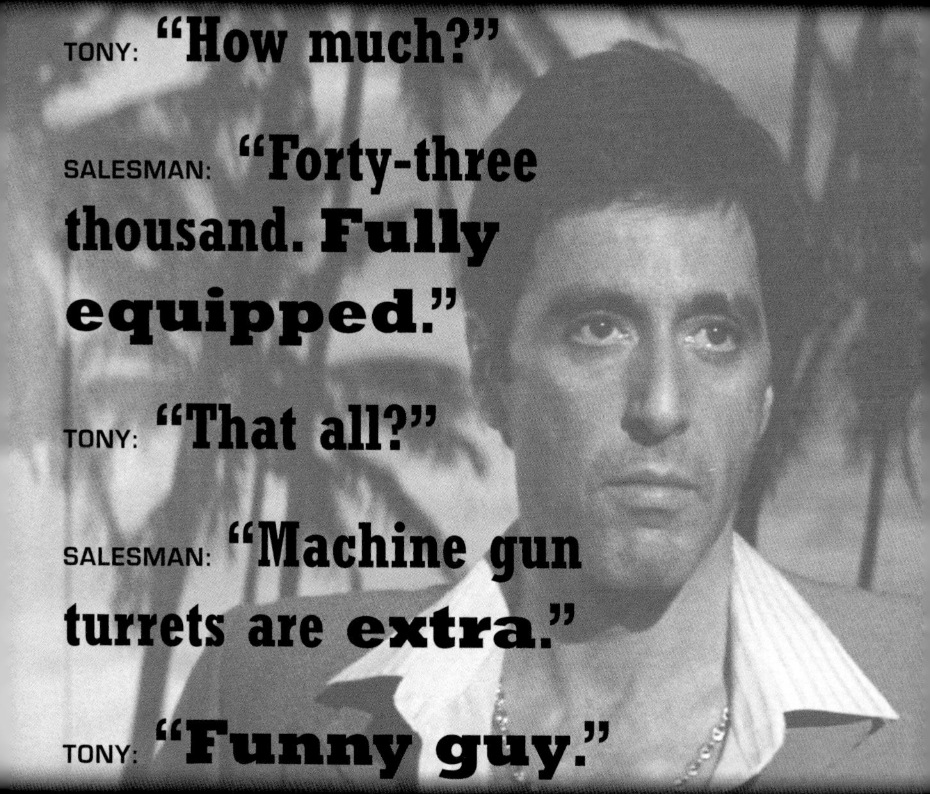

TONY: **"How much?"**

SALESMAN: **"Forty-three thousand. Fully equipped."**

TONY: **"That all?"**

SALESMAN: **"Machine gun turrets are extra."**

TONY: **"Funny guy."**

TONY: "Bulletproof this, okay? And this here . . . and the windows . . . . And get me one of them phones, y'know, with a scrambler. . . . And a radio with scanners, to pick out flying saucers, stuff like that. . . ."

ELVIRA: "Don't forget the fog lights."

TONY: "Oh, in case I get caught in the swamp. That's a good idea."

TONY: “That cable truck there. **Since when** does it take **three days** to rig a cable?”

MANNY: “**What**, you been watching it for three days?”

TONY: “The f#@%in’ thing has been there for three days! What am I gonna do, ***not* look** at it?”

LOPEZ: **"Tony . . . what happened to you?"**

TONY: **"They went and spoiled my eight-hundred-dollar suit."**

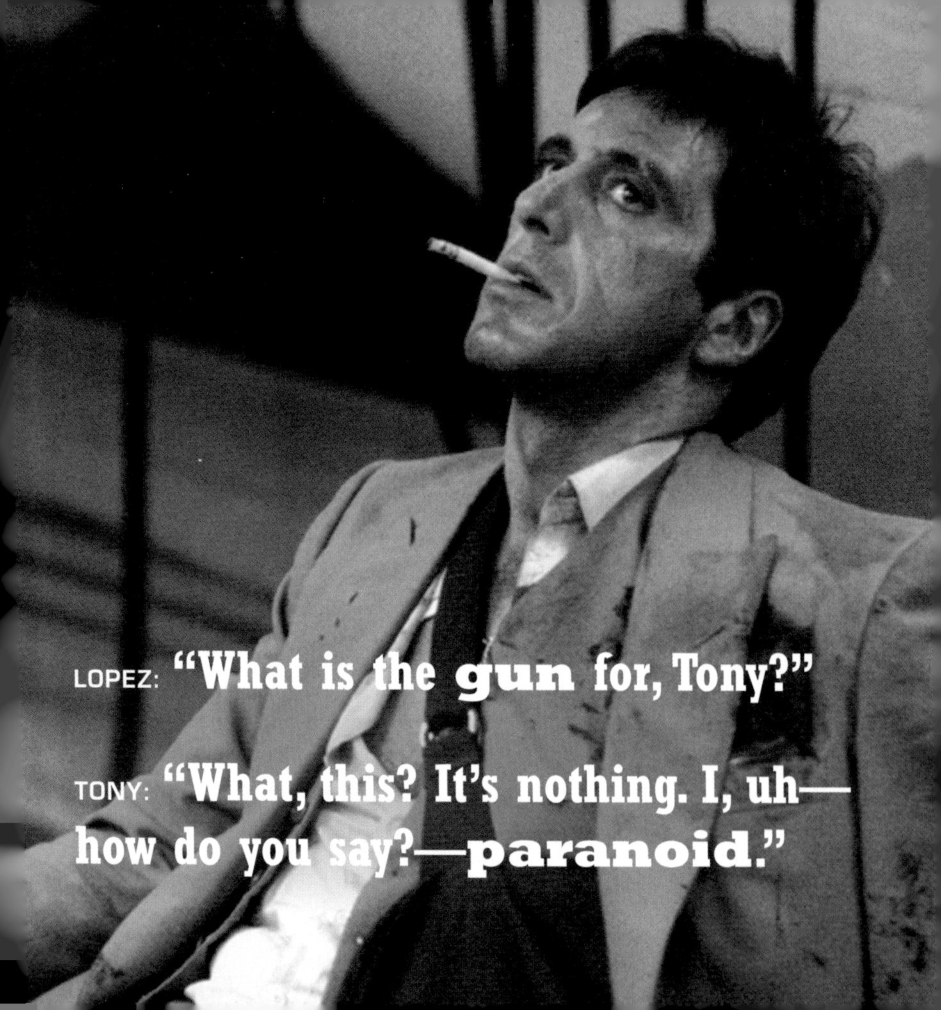

LOPEZ: “What is the **gun** for, Tony?”

TONY: “What, this? It’s nothing. I, uh—how do you say?—**paranoid**.”

TONY: "You wanna waste my time? Okay. I call my lawyer. He's the best lawyer in Miami. He's such a good lawyer that by tomorrow morning, you gonna be working in Alaska. So dress warm."

The Misunderstood

SCARFACE™

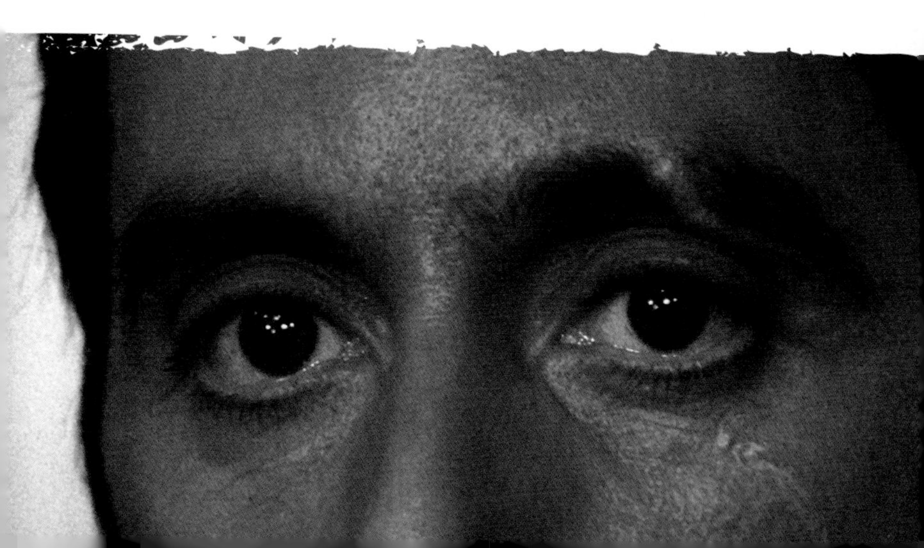

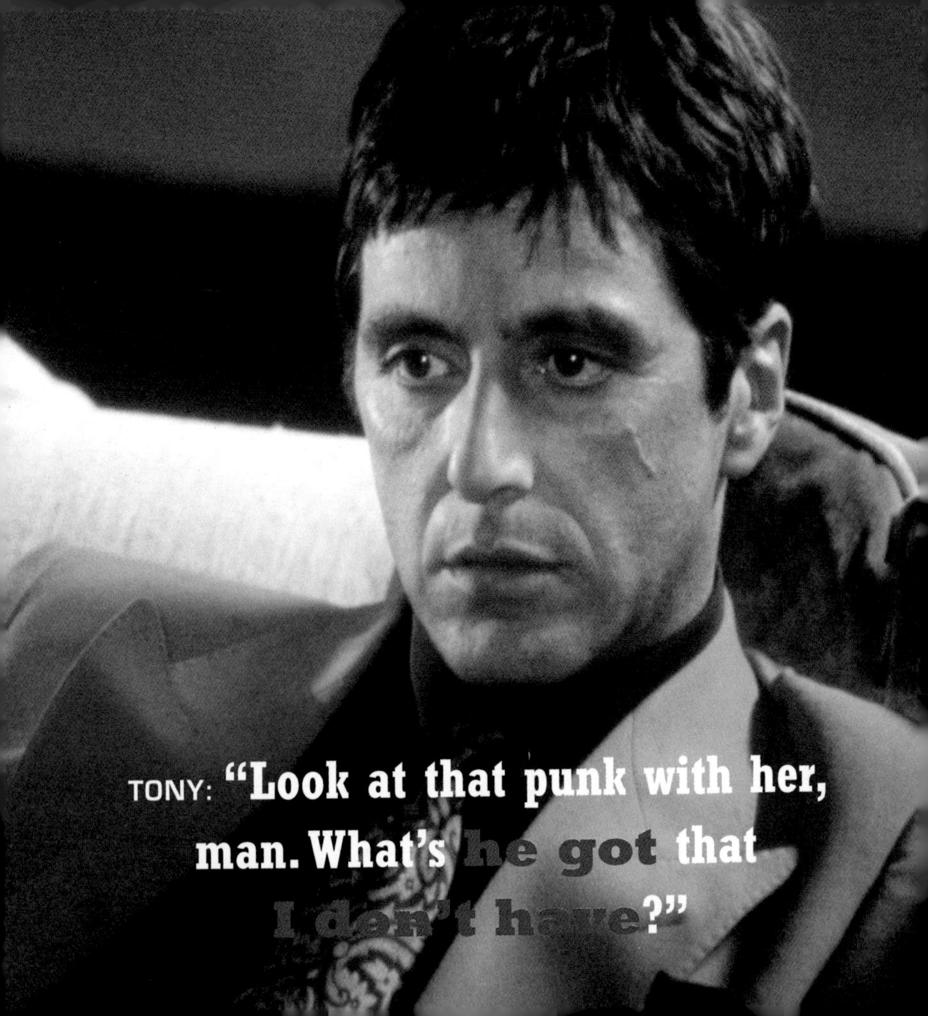
TONY: "Look at that punk with her, man. What's he got that I don't have?"

MANNY: "Well, he's very handsome, for one thing, you know. I mean, look at the way he dresses, man. Come on, that's *style*. Flash, pizzazz. And a little *coke money* doesn't hurt nobody, you know."

TONY: "You wanna have some ice cream? With my friend and me?"

BLONDE: "Get lost, **greaseball!**"

TONY: "You're **not** a negotiator, Manny, you **know** that. Come on, you like the ladies more than you like the money. That's **your** problem, okay?"

TONY: **"Somebody should do something about those—*those whores*. I mean, chargin' me ten points on my money. And they're getting away with it! F#@%, there's no laws anymore. I mean, anything goes."**

SHEFFIELD: "Tony, the law has to prove beyond a *reasonable* doubt. I'm an expert at raisin' that doubt. But when you got a million-three undeclared dollars staring into a videotape camera . . . honey, baby, it's hard to convince a jury you found it in a taxicab."

ELVIRA: **"Can't you see what we're becoming, Tony? We're *losers*. We're not winners; we're losers."**

TONY: "Go home. You're stoned."

TONY: "So what'd you tell 'em?"

MANNY: "I told them what **you told** me to tell them. I told them I was in sanitation. They didn't go for it."

TONY: "Sanitation? I told you to tell 'em you was in a ***sanitarium***, not sanitation. ***Sanitarium***."

The Prodigal

SCARFACE™

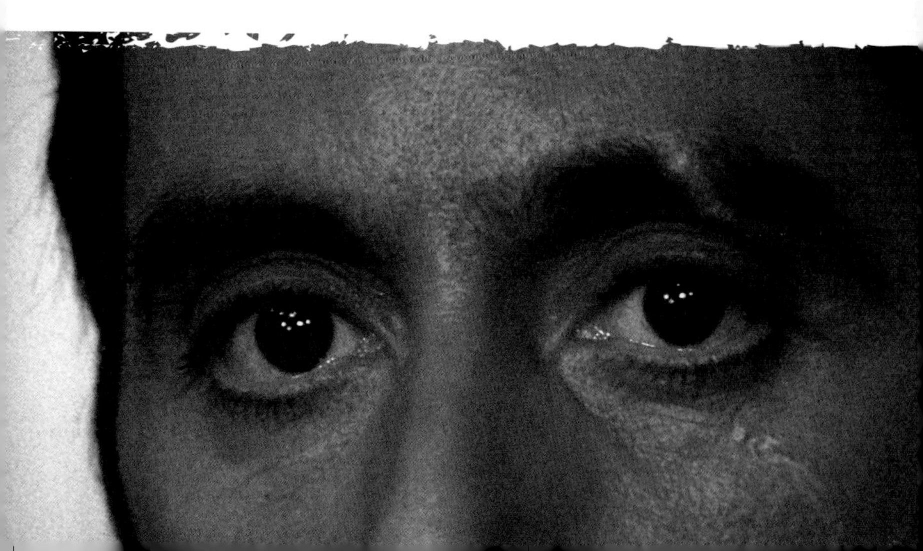

MANNY: "Man, you're **pushing** your luck . . ."

TONY: "*Mi hijo*, you worry too much. You're gonna have a **heart attack.**"

TONY: "Your son made it, *Mamá*. He's a success. That's why I didn't come around before. I want you to see what a good boy I been."

GINA: "It doesn't matter to me how long you've been away—five years or **ten** years. **You're my blood. Always.**"

MAMA: "Why do you have to **destroy** everything that comes your way?! ***¡Malagradecido! ¡Malino!***"

TONY:

“Gina. . . . Look at your face. It’s all dirty.”